A Cassava Republic Press edition 2017

First published in Belgium by De Eenhoorn
©Text and illustration: Mylo Freeman

Original Title: Prinses Arabella en de reuzentaart
Copyright 2014 by Uitgeverij De Eenhoorn, Vlasstraat 17, B-8710 Wielsbeke
(Belgium)

English Translation copyright © Laura Watkinson, 2017

ISBN 978-1-911115-42-7

A CIP catalogue record for this book is available from the British Library.

www.cassavarepublic.biz

Mylo Freeman

Princess Arabella
and the Giant Cake

CASSAVA REPUBLIC

Princess Arabella wants to have a **party!**
"My birthday party was so much fun..."
She laughs and shakes her curly head.
"And now... I want to have my birthday all over again!"

Her mum and dad didn't hear what she said.
"Hello?! Mum?! Dad?!" shouts Princess Arabella.
"I want to have my birthday all over again!"

"My dearest Arabella," Dad laughs. "You've only just had a birthday. You'll have to wait another year."
Hmph! That's no fun, is it?
"But someone else is about to have a birthday," her mum says. "In just a couple of days!"

Hmm... Who could it be?

Princess Arabella frowns and thinks very hard.
Is it Prince Mimoun? Or her lovely nanny, Ushio?
Or is it her favourite footman's birthday?

Of course! Now she remembers.

Princess Arabella laughs and claps her hands.

It's almost Grandma's birthday!

And Grandma is the nicest grandmother in the whole world.

Princess Ling, Princess Sophie and Prince Mimoun love her

just as much as Princess Arabella does.

"I'm going to bake a cake for Grandma,"

says Princess Ling, with a sparkle in her eyes. "A really, really yummy cake!"

"Hah!" says Prince Mimoun. "I'm going to bake a cake that's even yummier."

"No, you're not!" laughs Princess Sophie. "And I'm going to bake the biggest cake ever!"

Princess Arabella giggles.

"Well, the cake I'm going to bake will be the **yummiest** and the **biggest** cake ever in the whole wide world! Just you wait and see!"

With his mum's help, Prince Mimoun bakes a fabulous cake.
Mmm, so yummy! Prince Mimoun feels very proud.

Princess Sophie is busily working away too.

She secretly has a little taste.

Mmm, so yummy!

Princess Ling and her dad make a wonderful
Chinese cherry cake.
Mmm, so yummy!

It's the big day.

It's Grandma's birthday!

She can't believe her eyes.

So many yummy cakes!

"I'll never be able to eat them all," laughs Grandma.

Then she sees Princess Arabella's cake.

"Wow," sighs Grandma. "That must be the **biggest** and the **yummiest** cake ever in the whole wide world!"

"Just a second, Grandma!" cries Prince Mimoun. "Our cake isn't finished yet!"

What is Prince Mimoun planning?

He whispers something in Princess Ling's ear.
And then Princess Ling whispers in Princess Sophie's ear.
They quietly pile up their cakes, one on top of the other.

"Ha!" says Prince Mimoun.
"Now our cake is even bigger than Princess Arabella's."

It's time for Grandma to taste her cakes!
One big bite of every cake.
Which one will she like the best?
Prince Mimoun, Princess Sophie
and Princess Ling hold their breath.
But halfway through a bite of cake,
Grandma stops.
She looks around in surprise.

Hmm, that's strange...
Where is Princess Arabella?

Princess Arabella was hiding inside the giant cake!
Happy birthday, Grandma!

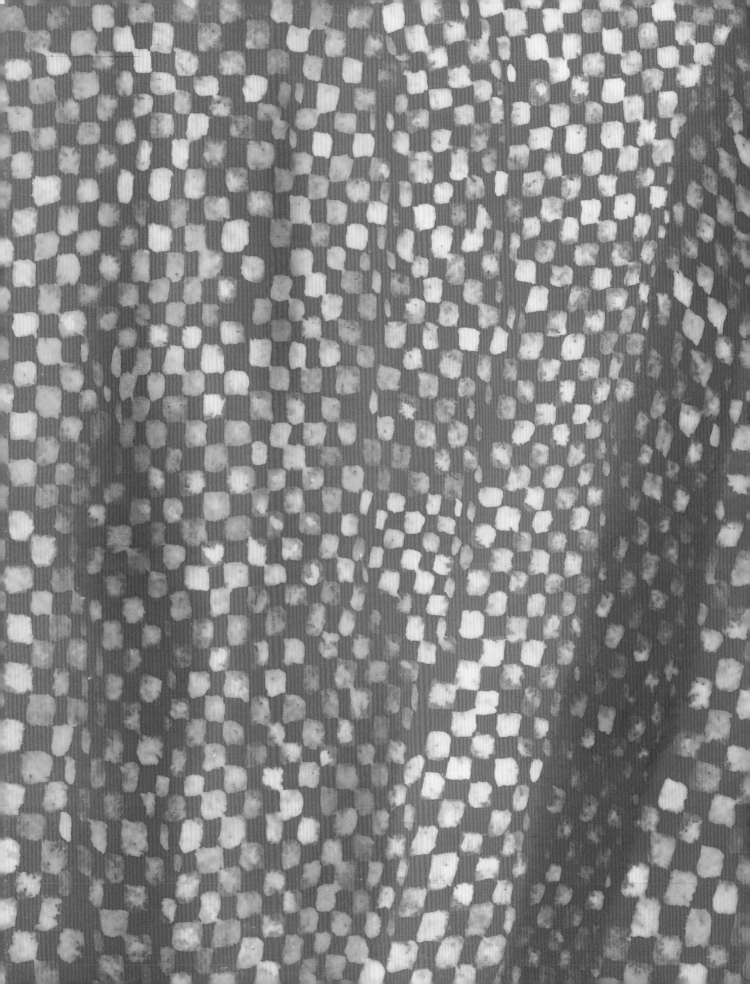